TOP 10
JOCKEYS

Betsy Kuhn

SPORTS
TOP 10

 Enslow Publishers, Inc.

40 Industrial Road	PO Box 38
Box 398	Aldershot
Berkeley Heights, NJ 07922	Hants GU12 6BP
USA	UK

http://www.enslow.com

Acknowledgments

The author would like to thank the following people for their help on this book: Tom Gilcoyne, National Museum of Racing and Hall of Fame; Kathy Heitz, Breeders' Cup Limited; Peggy Hendershot, National Thoroughbred Racing Association; Greg, Mom, and my winning exacta, Michael and Nicholas.

Copyright © 1999 by Betsy Kuhn

Library of Congress Cataloging-in-Publication Data

Kuhn, Betsy.
    Top 10 Jockeys / Betsy Kuhn.
        p. cm. — (Sports top 10)
    Includes bibliographical references (p. 46) and index.
    Summary: Presents the careers of ten notable jockeys in horse racing history, from the pioneers of thoroughbred racing to the most recent Kentucky Derby winners.
        ISBN 0-7660-1130-5
        1. Jockeys—United States—Biography—Juvenile literature.
    [1. Jockeys.] I. Title. II. Title: Top ten jockeys. III. Series.
    SF336.A2K78 1999
    798.4'0092'273—dc21
    [B]   98-44952
                                                                              CIP
                                                                               AC
Printed in the United States of America

10 9 8 7 6 5 4 3 2 1

To Our Readers:
All Internet addresses in this book were active and appropriate when we went to press. Any comments or suggestions can be sent by e-mail to Comments@ enslow.com or to the address on the back cover.

Illustration Credits: Bob Coglianese, pp. 6, 9, 14, 17, 25, 30, 33, 38; Breeders' Cup Photo, pp. 10, 13, 19, 22, 27, 41, 43; Double J Photos, pp. 29, 45; Jim Raftery-Turfotos, p. 21; Keeneland Library, p. 34; The Center of Excellence for the Study of Kentucky African Americans, Kentucky State University, p. 37.

Cover Illustration: Breeders' Cup Photo.

Cover Description: Gary Stevens: Champion, 1998 Belmont Stakes.

Interior Design: Richard Stalzer.

CONTENTS

INTRODUCTION

JOCKEYS DO MORE than simply ride horses. These amazing athletes face challenges and dangers unknown in other sports. Weighing little more than a hundred pounds on average, the jockey—balancing in two tiny stirrups—must control a powerful thoroughbred. A thoroughbred is a light, speedy horse bred for racing, yet it often weighs more than a thousand pounds. Jockeys ride these horses at speeds of up to 40 miles per hour, yet must steer them safely amid every other horse and jockey in the race. The risk of injury is so great that an ambulance follows the jockeys around the track.

The challenges do not begin and end with the dangers. Jockeys must keep incredibly fit to control their powerful mounts; that is, the horses they ride. Yet, at the same time, they must maintain their light weight. Also, they don't enjoy the off-season vacations that come with playing professional football or baseball. Most jockeys ride year-round, often six days a week.

A jockey must make split-second decisions while traveling at blazing speeds. The starting gate flies open; should the jockey take the horse to the rail or drop back? A jockey who doesn't hustle could end up outside a wall of horses and lose valuable ground. Does the jockey ask the horse for more speed on the backstretch or take on the competition at the turn? If the jockey asks for more speed too soon, the horse could tire early. Wait a second too long, and the horse could lose by a nose. A gap opens between horses; does the jockey shoot for the opening? In races that often last little more than a minute, the jockey must react quickly.

All jockeys start out as apprentices. During the apprenticeship, a jockey races with a weight allowance of five to ten pounds—that is, the jockey's horse carries less total weight than those of the more experienced riders. A lower weight often improves a horse's chances of winning, which encourages owners to use these less experienced riders. When the apprenticeship is over, the jockey becomes a journeyman rider.

Not everyone may agree on who the top jockeys are. One thing that can be agreed upon, though, is the fact that the top jockeys have what it takes to reach the winner's circle again and again. They dominate the prestigious Triple Crown races, which are the Kentucky Derby, the Preakness Stakes, and the Belmont Stakes. They reign supreme on Breeders' Cup Day, the Super Bowl of thoroughbred racing. Held every year in the late fall, the eight Breeders' Cup races draw the world's best horses and jockeys.

The ten jockeys profiled in *our* list are among the best of that group, and will long be remembered for their accomplishments in thoroughbred racing.

CAREER STATISTICS

JOCKEY	CAREER	STARTS	WINS
EDDIE ARCARO	1931–61	24,092	4,779
JERRY BAILEY	1974–	25,297	4,472
STEVE CAUTHEN*	1976–93	5,069	954
ANGEL CORDERO, JR.	1960–92	38,646	7,057
PAT DAY	1973–	33,741	7,387
KENT DESORMEAUX	1986–	18,135	3,721
JULIE KRONE	1981–99	20,242	3,503
ISAAC MURPHY	1875–95	1,412	628
BILL SHOEMAKER	1949–90	40,350	8,833
GARY STEVENS	1979–	25,092	4,443

Statistics are as of February 20, 1999.
*Excludes European racing.

EDDIE ARCARO

With his win on Citation in the 1948 Belmont Stakes, Eddie Arcaro became the first thoroughbred jockey to win two Triple Crowns.

BEFORE THE START OF THE 1948 Belmont Stakes, jockey Eddie Arcaro was feeling pretty confident. He and his mount, Citation, had already won the Kentucky Derby and the Preakness Stakes by a combined nine lengths. Now he declared, "The only way I can lose this race is if I fall off my horse."[1] Sure enough, when the starting gate flew open, Citation stumbled and Arcaro nearly fell off. By the time he righted himself, the rest of the field was nothing but a cloud of thundering hooves ahead of them. But Arcaro and Citation easily overtook the field to win by an awe-inspiring eight lengths, sweeping the Triple Crown and giving Arcaro his second Triple Crown victory, a record unmatched to this day.

No doubt Arcaro would give all the credit for the win to Citation, whom he called the best three-year-old colt he had ever ridden (a colt is a male horse under the age of five). He was always quick to point out the difference good horses made to a jockey's success. But The Master, as Arcaro was known, would not have earned the mounts on such talented horses had he not been such a phenomenal talent himself.

Born George Edward Arcaro in 1916 in Cincinnati, Ohio, he began his thoroughbred racing career at age thirteen, working as an exercise rider at a racetrack near his home. After he began racing at fifteen, it took him eight months to win his first race. Yet trainer Clarence Davison recognized his potential, signed him as a rider for fifty dollars a month, and gave him plenty of mounts. In 1938, Arcaro won his first Kentucky Derby on a colt called Lawrin, eventually winning the Derby a record-setting five times.

He won his second Derby in 1941 on Whirlaway, then rode the colt to a Triple Crown victory. In 1948, he got the mount on Citation when the colt's regular rider disappeared on a fishing trip in Florida, never to be found. Before the Derby, Arcaro wondered whether he should have chosen to ride Citation's swift stablemate, Coaltown, who was also running.

When Coaltown left the gate in a burst of speed, Arcaro was sure he was on the wrong horse. "But," he said, "when I asked Citation to run, he shot past Coaltown and everybody else with ease."[2]

In 1955, he lost the Derby aboard Nashua, the favorite, to Swaps, ridden by Bill Shoemaker. After Arcaro and Nashua came back to beat Swaps in the Preakness and Belmont Stakes, the two colts met for a match race in Chicago to settle the score for good. "Look at this colt's head now," Arcaro told Shoemaker. "When that gate opens, all you're going to see is his rear end."[3] Sure enough, Nashua won by more than six lengths.

Fans adored the highly competitive Arcaro not only for his considerable riding skills, but also for his outgoing, winning personality. They lovingly dubbed him Banana Nose. Out of concern for his fellow jockeys, Arcaro helped found the Jockeys' Guild and later served as the Guild's president. The Guild serves as an advocacy group, furthering jockeys' causes, and giving financial and medical aid to needy members and their families.

By the time Arcaro retired in 1961, he was a legend. He remained fun-loving into old age, even breaking a leg at age seventy, sliding down a banister. When he died in 1997, Joe Hirsch, a racing columnist for *Daily Racing Form*, said, "He's the best I ever saw, and I think he's the best anybody ever saw. He was a combination of strength and smarts and his sense of daring was unmatched."[4]

EDDIE ARCARO

BORN: February 19, 1916, Cincinnati, Ohio.
DIED: November 14, 1997, Miami, Florida.
FIRST WINNER: Eagle Bird, January 14, 1932, Agua Caliente, Mexico.
HEIGHT: Five feet three inches.
IMPORTANT WINS: Kentucky Derby, 1938, 1941, 1945, 1948, 1952;
    Preakness Stakes, 1941, 1948, 1950–1951, 1955, 1957; Belmont
    Stakes, 1941–1942, 1945, 1948, 1952, 1955; won two Triple
    Crowns, in 1941 and 1948.
HONORS: Inducted into the National Museum of Racing's Hall of
    Fame in 1958.

Eddie Arcaro rides Nashua to victory in the 1955 Dwyer Stakes.

Internet Address
http://hall.racingmuseum.org/jockey.asp?ID=16

JERRY BAILEY

Jerry Bailey won his fourth Breeders' Cup Classic in 1995 on Cigar.

JERRY BAILEY HAD NEVER BEEN one to get too attached to the horses he rode. Then, in 1994, he got the mount on a horse named Cigar. First, they won the NYRA Mile at Aqueduct by seven lengths. Then, they went to Florida and won three races in a row at Gulfstream Park. When they raced in the Oaklawn Handicap in Arkansas, another rider accidentally struck Cigar with his whip. Looking as if he were angry, Cigar shot ahead by a couple of strides, winning with gritty determination. He kept winning race after race; nothing could dampen his fighting spirit. Then, in the 1996 Dubai World Cup, he was leading the field when Soul of the Matter passed him with a powerful move in the stretch. Cigar looked beat. But with one last grueling surge of energy, he came on again to win the race. Eventually, with Bailey in the saddle, he won sixteen races in a row, tying Citation's 1950 record. For the first time, Bailey grew attached to a horse, perhaps because he saw in Cigar something of his own competitive spirit.

From the time he was a kid growing up in El Paso, Texas, Bailey loved to compete. But, he said, "I was too small for football, too short for basketball, and too slow for track."[1] His future began to take shape when he was eleven, when his father, a dentist, bought some quarterhorses. Soon Bailey was working in the barns, cleaning stalls, and exercising horses—even riding in match races. By seventeen, he was riding thoroughbreds, winning with his first mount, Fetch, at New Mexico's Sunland Park.

After his high school graduation, Bailey began riding at various tracks around the country, including Florida, where he won several riding titles. In 1982, he moved his *tack*—another term for stable gear—to New York, home to one of the country's best and most competitive jockey colonies. Soon he was piling on more riding titles.

Bailey is known as a thinking man's jockey, an intelligent rider who wins by using his head as much as his physical strength. That intelligence, along with his fine sense of pace, has helped him win the Breeders' Cup Classic a record four times, starting with the 1991 Classic on Black Tie Affair. Bailey controlled the race from the start. He sent Black Tie Affair to the lead. Then Bailey slowed down the pace, saving the horse's energy for the stretch drive—the final leg of the race. As they neared the finish, Bailey asked Black Tie Affair for more speed. By now, the other horses couldn't catch up, and he hit the wire first.

In the 1993 Classic, Bailey rode a French horse named Arcangues who was racing on the dirt, instead of turf, for the very first time. Before reaching the paddock (the area where the horses are saddled), he did not even know how to pronounce the horse's name (Ar-Kong). But, said Bailey, "He ran like King Kong,"[2] and he stunned the racing world by guiding the horse to a win at odds of 133 to 1.

Bailey won the Kentucky Derby aboard Sea Hero in 1993; and he won again in 1996, when he thrilled racing fans with his come-from-behind finish on Grindstone. In 1997, racing columnist Joe Hirsch said that Bailey was "riding as good, or better, than anybody in the country. Maybe the world."[3]

Bailey served as president of the Jockeys' Guild for seven years. During his presidency, he lobbied hard for safety measures such as the protective vest that saved Julie Krone's life in a 1993 accident.

JERRY BAILEY

BORN: August 29, 1957, Dallas, Texas.

FIRST WINNER: Fetch, November 1974, Sunland Park, New Mexico.

HEIGHT: Five feet five inches.

IMPORTANT WINS: Kentucky Derby, 1993, 1996; Preakness Stakes, 1991; Belmont Stakes, 1991; seven Breeders' Cup wins, including four Classics.

HONORS: Inducted into the National Museum of Racing's Hall of Fame in 1995; Eclipse Award: Outstanding Jockey, 1995–1997.

Bailey stunned racing fans by winning the 1993 Breeders' Cup Classic on Arcangues, a horse considered to be a long shot.

Internet Address

http://hall.racingmuseum.org/jockey.asp?ID=164

STEVE CAUTHEN

Steve Cauthen rode Affirmed (on right) to a thrilling victory over Alydar in the 1978 Belmont Stakes.

THE NIGHT BEFORE HE WAS TO RIDE in the 1978 Kentucky Derby, eighteen-year-old Steve Cauthen slept on the floor of the hotel room he was sharing with his family, because his younger brothers said it was their turn for the bed. The next day, Cauthen got up off the floor and won the Derby on Affirmed, beating their rival, Alydar, by a length and a half. Two weeks later, they beat Alydar by a neck in the Preakness Stakes.

Now they were facing each other once more in the Belmont Stakes. As Cauthen steered Affirmed to the top of the long Belmont stretch, it was clear that they were in for the race of their lives. On their outside, pinning them close to the rail, was Alydar, with Jorge Velasquez in the saddle. Alydar was running as if he were determined to avenge his prior losses. Neck-and-neck the colts fought each other for the lead down the stretch, with Alydar pressing Affirmed so close to the rail that Cauthen had no room to use the whip right-handed. So, for the first time ever, he hit Affirmed on the left. In a thrilling finish, they won the race by a head, making Cauthen the youngest jockey ever to win the Triple Crown.

Steve Cauthen, nicknamed The Kid, grew up in a horse-loving family in Walton, Kentucky. His father, Tex, a blacksmith, had once dreamed of being a jockey; his mother and two uncles were horse trainers. By the time Cauthen was twelve, he knew he wanted to be a jockey. In the loft of his family's barn, he practiced riding on a saddle strapped to a bale of hay, holding the reins and switching the whip, just as his father had taught him. He watched tapes of races from River Downs, and he and his father visited the racetrack to study riders leaving the starting gate.

Five days after he began riding, at age sixteen, Cauthen won for the first time on Red Pipe at River Downs, then went on to win the track's riding title. After that, there was no stopping him. He won 240 races that year, a record for an apprentice. He topped that by winning 487 races in 1977, including twenty-three in one week. That year, he was named Sportsman of the Year by *Sports Illustrated*. By the time he swept the Triple Crown, Cauthen was a household name.

That winter, he switched his tack to Southern California. But the trainers there preferred to use their regular jockeys, not some hotshot kid from the East. Unable to secure good mounts, Cauthen fell into a horrible slump, going 110 races without a win. As a result, he lost the mount on Affirmed.

What's more, because he was young, he was still growing, making it difficult for him to maintain a low weight. When a well-to-do English owner asked him to ride in Europe, where jockeys are generally heavier, he moved to England, where he was the leading rider in 1984, 1985, and 1987. By the time he retired in 1993, he was the only jockey ever to have won the Kentucky, Irish, French, Italian, and English Derbies.

Cauthen "was just one with the horse . . ." remembers jockey Pat Day, "and even when he was asking for their best, it wasn't an aggressive, visible thing." What's more, with all the media attention he endured, he was "totally unflappable."[1]

STEVE CAUTHEN

BORN: May 1, 1960, Covington, Kentucky.

FIRST WINNER: Red Pipe, May 17, 1976, River Downs, Ohio.

HEIGHT: Five feet six inches.

IMPORTANT WINS: Kentucky Derby, 1978; Preakness Stakes, 1978; Belmont Stakes, 1978; Triple Crown, 1978.

HONORS: Eclipse Award: Award of Merit, 1977; Eclipse Award: Outstanding Jockey, 1977; Eclipse Award: Outstanding Apprentice Jockey, 1977; inducted into the National Museum of Racing's Hall of Fame in 1994.

In 1978, aboard Affirmed, Steve Cauthen became the youngest jockey to ever win the Triple Crown.

Internet Address

http://hall.racingmuseum.org/jockey.asp?ID=175

GOING INTO THE 1976 KENTUCKY DERBY, Angel Cordero, Jr., felt his chances on Bold Forbes were pretty good. Bold Forbes was a speedy colt who liked to race near the front of the pack. So did his main rival, Honest Pleasure. But Honest Pleasure's jockey was a conservative rider. Cordero guessed that he would keep Honest Pleasure under a firm hold and save some run for the stretch drive. Thus, when the gates flew open, Cordero hustled Bold Forbes to a five-length lead. Honest Pleasure, kept to a more measured pace, never had a chance. Bold Forbes won, thanks to a ride that was typical of Cordero: smart and aggressive. These traits helped Cordero become one of the winningest jockeys ever.

Cordero, born in Puerto Rico in 1942, was the son of a jockey-turned-trainer and grew up on the grounds of a race-track. In 1960, three days into his career, he won his first race aboard Celador at El Comandante racetrack. A year later, he was the track's leading rider.

In 1962, he moved to the United States. He spent his first summer in Saratoga Springs, New York, where he had trouble getting mounts at Saratoga Race Course. The apartment he rented for seventy-five dollars a week with two other men had only two beds. One man did the cooking so he got one of the beds, but Cordero and the other man had to roll dice to see who got to sleep on the second bed. Cordero often ended up sleeping in his car.

Cordero was homesick and spoke no English. Eventually, he became so discouraged that he returned to Puerto Rico to ride. But he came back to the States in 1966

ANGEL CORDERO, JR.

In 1988, Angel Cordero, Jr., became the first jockey to win back-to-back Breeders' Cup races. He rode Gulch to victory in the Sprint, and won the Juvenile Fillies on Open Mind.

with renewed confidence, and by 1968, he was the country's leading rider. He seemed especially determined to win at Saratoga, perhaps because he had found such an unfriendly welcome at this posh racing haven that first year. He won the Saratoga riding title in 1967, and then went on to win it a remarkable twelve more times.

His success carried over to Churchill Downs where he won his first Kentucky Derby on Cannonade in 1974 and his third Derby on Spend A Buck in 1985. By now he was known as a rider who wanted to win more than anything. Once, a trainer told him that his horse would run faster if Cordero would say, "Run, Sparky, run." Cordero was already one of the most winning jockeys in the country; still, he urged the horse, "Run, Sparky, run!" (They still lost by a nose.) Fans loved Cordero, not simply because he gave his all in every race, but also because of his enthusiasm, his big, bright smile, and his trademark leaping dismount in the winner's circle.

In 1991, he won his seven thousandth race. Then, in a 1992 riding accident at Aqueduct, Cordero suffered injuries so serious that doctors warned him another spill could be fatal. That May, with tears in his eyes, he announced his retirement. He left as the nation's third winningest jockey, behind only Bill Shoemaker and Laffit Pincay, Jr.

After his racing career ended, Cordero worked as a trainer for several years. He then became an agent for up-and-coming jockey John Velazquez. With Cordero's expert support, Velazquez won the 1998 Saratoga riding title.

When describing Cordero, "one thing stands out: Wanting to win at all costs, wanting to win more than anybody," said trainer Nick Zito. "He is, without a doubt, one of the greatest competitors I've ever witnessed in my life."[1]

ANGEL CORDERO, JR.

BORN: November 8, 1942, Santurce, Puerto Rico.

FIRST WINNER: Celador, June 15, 1960, El Comandante Racetrack, Puerto Rico.

HEIGHT: Five feet three inches.

IMPORTANT WINS: Kentucky Derby, 1974, 1976, 1985; Preakness Stakes, 1980, 1984; Belmont Stakes, 1976; four Breeders' Cup wins.

HONORS: Eclipse Award: Outstanding Jockey, 1982–1983; inducted into the National Museum of Racing's Hall of Fame, 1988.

Cordero celebrated his 6,000th win with his trademark leaping dismount.

Internet Address

http://hall.racingmuseum.org/jockey.asp?ID=177

PAT DAY

Pat Day salutes the heavens after winning the first Breeders' Cup Classic in 1984 on Wild Again.

AS THE GATES FLEW OPEN for the 1992 Kentucky Derby, the crowd was focused on Arazi, a horse touted to be the next Secretariat. Few fans were watching Pat Day aboard Lil E. Tee, who was going off at odds of 16 to 1. Day was the Churchill Downs leading rider of all time, but in nine tries, he had never won the Derby. In the 1987 Derby, he had chosen to ride Demons Begone instead of Alysheba; Alysheba won. In 1990, he had opted for the mount on Summer Squall instead of Unbridled; Unbridled won. Two other times, he had come in second. As Day watched Arazi fly past him on the backstretch, he thought his Derby dreams had fizzled once more.

At the top of the stretch, though, Arazi began to tire. Day, just two lengths behind, asked Lil E. Tee for run, that is, to quicken his gallop. They soon put the rest of the field behind them to hit the wire first. Pat Day had won the Run for the Roses (the Kentucky Derby) at last, and he thanked Lil E. Tee with a peppermint.

When Day was growing up in the ranching community of Eagle, Colorado, he never dreamed of winning the Derby. Rather, he longed to ride on the rodeo circuit. He honed his skills in Little Britches Rodeo and on the high school rodeo team. At age nineteen, he began racing thoroughbreds and notched his first win aboard Forblunged at Arizona's Prescott Downs in 1973. In 1982, he won more races than any other jockey in the United States.

But, despite his success, he felt something was missing in his life. He began abusing drugs and alcohol. Then, on the night of January 27, 1984, in a Miami hotel room, he turned on the TV to find evangelist Jimmy Swaggart preaching. Day turned off the set and fell asleep. When he woke up later, he felt what he described as a presence in the room, which he now believes was the Holy Spirit. He turned on the TV and saw Swaggart just completing his call to the altar. At that moment, Day turned his life over to Jesus Christ. For a time, he considered giving up racing for the ministry. But, after struggling with the question, he felt that God had given him his riding talent for a purpose.[1]

That year, Day won the very first Breeders' Cup Classic on a long shot named Wild Again. When he reached the winner's circle and was about to salute the crowd, he heard a voice say, "It's not them, but Me."[2] He whisked off his helmet and thrust it skyward. He has since gone on to win more races on Breeders' Cup Day than any other jockey, including the 1998 Breeders' Cup Classic on Awesome Again.

Often nicknamed Patient Pat or Pat "Wait All" Day, he is known for driving fans crazy by waiting until the last possible moment to ask his mount to run. Then Day thrills them when his horse hits the finish line in the nick of time. But patience has paid off for Day. In 1997, he won his seven thousandth race, one of only five jockeys ever to reach this milestone. As is his way, he took none of the glory for himself, saying simply, "I'm grateful that God gave me the ability and opportunities to do this."[3]

PAT DAY

BORN: October 13, 1953, Brush, Colorado.

FIRST WINNER: Forblunged, August 29, 1973, Prescott Downs, Arizona.

HEIGHT: Five feet eleven inches.

IMPORTANT WINS: Kentucky Derby, 1992; Preakness Stakes, 1985, 1990, 1994–1996; Belmont Stakes, 1989, 1994; ten Breeders' Cup wins.

HONORS: Eclipse Award: Outstanding Jockey, 1984, 1986–1987, 1991; inducted into the National Museum of Racing's Hall of Fame in 1991.

Pat Day rode Easy Goer to an impressive win in the 1989 Belmont Stakes. Day has called Easy Goer the best horse he's ever ridden.

Internet Address

http://hall.racingmuseum.org/jockey.asp?ID=179

KENT DESORMEAUX

Kent Desormeaux won the 1993 Breeders' Cup Turf race aboard Kotashaan.

KENT DESORMEAUX

As Post Time Drew Near for the 1998 Kentucky Derby, Kent Desormeaux, in red-and-gold silks, guided his mount, Real Quiet, into the starting gate. It had been ten years since Desormeaux had first ridden in the Derby. Back then, he was the hottest young jockey in the country. Since that time, he'd seen his career skyrocket, then sag. Now, it seemed, he was having to prove himself all over again.

When the gates flew open, Desormeaux positioned Real Quiet on the rail, tucking him neatly behind the leaders. Then, on the backstretch, he took Real Quiet to the outside as he asked for more speed. A mile into the race, they'd seized the lead, and they never gave it up. As Desormeaux crossed the wire, he thrust his fist triumphantly in the air, screaming with happiness. "I feel so good inside, so good," he exclaimed.[1]

It had been a long journey to the Churchill Downs winner's circle for Desormeaux. He grew up in Louisiana's Cajun country, where he used to race his pony against motorcycles. He earned money for his first saddle by driving a tractor for two dollars an hour. His mother cried when he left home at sixteen to be a jockey, worried that he was too young to handle racetrack life. But Desormeaux, determined to ride, took off for Louisiana Downs. He stayed there only a few months before trying his luck in Maryland.

Success came almost immediately. Only seventeen years old and a fearless rider, as an apprentice he won more races in 1987 than any other jockey in the nation. In 1989, he won a record 598 races in one year. Ready for the big time, he moved his tack to Southern California. Although he was competing against some of the country's top riders, he'd claimed a riding title by 1990. At twenty-one, he became the youngest jockey ever to have won two thousand races. Nothing seemed to slow him down, not even a 1992 riding accident so serious that he lost the hearing in one ear. In three months, as daring as ever, he was racing again.

Desormeaux's early success gave him a confidence that some people interpreted as arrogance. By 1994, trainers were complaining that he did not listen to instructions. He seemed to grow careless. Suddenly, he wasn't winning as much. Critics noted that he didn't ride every horse to the wire; if he wasn't getting a good performance from his mount, he seemed to give up in the stretch. On the list of the top jockeys in California, his name was somewhere near the bottom.

"When I went from leading rider to falling off the end of the map," he said, "that was a slap in the face. I began to realize I'm not as good as I thought I was."[2]

In 1997, yearning to get back to the top of the standings, he worked hard to restore his reputation. But by then, some trainers had had enough of his arrogance. Trainer Bob Baffert gave him a chance, putting him on his horses, including Real Quiet, a colt that had once been so thin he was nicknamed The Fish.

Now Desormeaux and the Fish had repaid Baffert's faith in them by winning the 1998 Kentucky Derby. Two weeks later, they won the Preakness Stakes. They lost the Belmont Stakes, and their quest for the Triple Crown, by a heartbreaking nose. But Triple Crown or no Triple Crown, Desormeaux was back and at the top of his game.

KENT DESORMEAUX

BORN: February 27, 1970, Maurice, Louisiana.

FIRST WINNER: Miss Tavern, July 13, 1986, Evangeline Downs, Louisiana.

HEIGHT: Five feet three inches.

IMPORTANT WINS: Kentucky Derby, 1998; Preakness Stakes, 1998; two Breeders' Cup wins.

HONORS: Eclipse Award: Outstanding Apprentice Jockey, 1987; Eclipse Award: Outstanding Jockey, 1989, 1992.

A triumphant Kent Desormeaux returns to the winner's circle aboard Real Quiet after their 1998 Preakness Stakes win.

Internet Address

http://206.135.60.53/all_star/kent_desormeaux.html

JULIE KRONE

With her 1993 Belmont Stakes win on Colonial Affair, Julie Krone became the first woman to win a Triple Crown race.

JULIE KRONE

ON JUNE 5, 1993, Julie Krone guided Colonial Affair, a big bay colt, into the starting gate for the Belmont Stakes. Two years earlier, Krone had been the first woman to ride in this prestigious Triple Crown race. Today, her mount was full of spirit, and she felt they could win. As jockeys would say, Krone "had horse."

Colonial Affair broke quickly from the gate. On the backstretch, Krone moved him to the outside, and soon Colonial Affair was passing the nine horses in front of him, accelerating down the stretch. When he hit the wire first, Julie Krone became the first female jockey to win a Triple Crown race.

Other professional sports have separate leagues for women. But female jockeys have to compete head-to-head with their male competitors.

That never worried Julieann Louise Krone, who won her first ribbon in a horse show at age five. Her mother, Judi, was a dressage rider, and when little Julie would fall off a horse, Judi made sure she got right back on. But it was Filly, Krone's sly and spirited pony, who really taught her how to ride. They would ride for miles around the family farm in Eau Claire, Michigan, with Filly testing Krone at every step.

In 1978, when Krone saw Steve Cauthen win the Kentucky Derby on TV, she knew right away that she wanted to be a jockey. She began to practice race riding, draping a saddle over a bench and wielding a flyswatter as a whip. That summer, she worked at Churchill Downs as a hotwalker (one who cools down the horses after a race), groom, and exercise rider. The following summer she began racing quarterhorses at fair tracks in Michigan. At seventeen, she set off for Tampa, Florida, where her grandparents lived, to begin riding in earnest.

"So, little girl, you wanna be a jockey?" asked a trainer at Tampa Bay Downs. "No, sir, " Krone replied, "I'm *gonna* be a jockey."[1] She won her first thoroughbred race aboard Lord Farkle on February 12, 1981. Later, she rode as an apprentice in Maryland. Her career really took off in 1982, when she moved to New Jersey. Over the next eight years, she won four consecutive riding titles at The Meadowlands and three in a row at Monmouth Park. By now, trainers recognized how well she communicated with horses. She was known as having "good hands"—under her touch, a horse would relax and give its best performance. By 1990, she had switched her tack to New York, successfully taking on the East Coast's top riders.

A few months after her Belmont Stakes win, she was nearly killed when another horse bumped hers. Tossed from the saddle, she tumbled into the path of a horse that stamped on her chest. If not for her safety vest, the blow might have been fatal. Even so, she wound up with a bruised heart and a badly shattered ankle, requiring eight months of painful rehabilitation. A determined Krone returned to racing the following May, and in November 1995, she rode her three thousandth winner. She retired in April 1999 as the winningest female jockey ever.

Says Andrew Beyer of the *Washington Post*, "A good case can be made that Krone is the most remarkable female athlete of all time. Has there ever been a woman . . . in any other physical sport who could compete on even terms with the top male athletes? The only one who has ever done so is Julie Krone."[2]

JULIE KRONE

BORN: July 24, 1963, Benton Harbor, Michigan.

FIRST WINNER: Lord Farkle, February 12, 1981, Tampa Bay Downs, Florida.

HEIGHT: Four feet ten inches.

IMPORTANT WINS: Belmont Stakes, 1993.

In August, 1993, Julie Krone won five races in one day at Saratoga.

Internet Address

http://www.breederscup.com/champion/bios97/jockeys/krone.html

ISAAC MURPHY

Isaac Murphy won 44 percent of his races, a mark that has never been equaled.

IT WAS THE MATCH RACE OF THE YEAR: June 25, 1890. Isaac Murphy was riding the great colt Salvator, against the colt's rival, Tenny, and his jockey, Edward "Snapper" Garrison. As the race began, Murphy sat as still as a stone, letting his mount pull ahead by two lengths with his strong, sure strides. As Salvator picked up the pace, Garrison put the whip to Tenny, urging him on. Murphy remained calm. Again and again, Garrison used the whip, frantically asking his colt for more run. Finally, they began to gain on Murphy and Salvator. Glancing behind him, Murphy saw them coming, faster and faster. Fans waited desperately for him to react—to pick up his whip. But, merely leaning forward, he rode Salvator to the wire, to win by a head.

The win was typical of the unshakable Isaac Murphy. A racing newspaper summed up his style by saying, "No man with a touch of heart disease should ever back his mounts."[1] With his patience and skill, he won over 44 percent of his starts, a winning percentage that remains unmatched to this day.[2]

Isaac Burns (his name at birth) was born in Kentucky just before the Civil War. His father, a freeman bricklayer, joined the Union army. He died a prisoner in a Confederate camp, not far from his home. After the war, Isaac's mother moved the family to Lexington to live with her father, Green Murphy, whose surname Isaac later adopted. While Isaac's mother was working as a laundress, one of her employers noticed that Isaac was small for his age. The employer referred Murphy to his partner, who took him on as an apprentice jockey when Murphy was twelve. Working with trainer Eli Jordan, Murphy began racing in 1875, the year of the first Kentucky Derby.

At that time, African-American jockeys and trainers were a major force in the thoroughbred world. They had been since before the Civil War, when the South was home to some of the country's most successful stables. Of the first twenty-eight Kentucky Derbies, African-American jockeys won fifteen of them, three of which were won by Murphy.

He won his first Derby in 1884 aboard Buchanan, a horse so testy that just before the race, he threw Murphy off his back. When the race started, Murphy felt compelled to keep the high-spirited colt under a tight hold. He didn't even reach for his whip, yet they reached the finish line first. Murphy won the Derby again in 1890 and 1891, making him the first jockey to win the Derby three times, and the first to land back-to-back wins.

His sense of pace was uncanny. A horse owner once asked him to ride his colt, Ban Fox, against Bankrupt, who was on a winning streak. He told Murphy to reach the quarter pole in twenty-four and a half seconds, the half pole in forty-nine seconds, and to complete the race in one minute, fourteen and a half seconds. The owner later reported that Murphy had ridden Ban Fox to victory exactly as instructed, right to the last half second.

In the Louisville, Kentucky, *Courier-Journal* in 1891, it said, "[Isaac Murphy's] integrity and honor are the pride of the turf, and many of the best horsemen pronounce him the greatest jockey that ever mounted a horse."[3] Murphy's stellar career was cut short when he died of pneumonia in his mid-thirties.

ISAAC MURPHY

BORN: January 1, Fayette County, Kentucky. Murphy's birthyear is unknown. Historians believe he was born anywhere from 1858 to 1861.

DIED: February 12, 1896, Lexington, Kentucky.

FIRST WINNER: Glentina, September 15, 1876, Crab Orchard Racetrack, Kentucky.

HEIGHT: About five feet.

IMPORTANT WINS: Kentucky Derby, 1884, 1890–1891.

HONORS: First jockey inducted into the National Museum of Racing's Hall of Fame, 1955.

Isaac Murphy became the first jockey to win the Kentucky Derby three times.

Internet Address

http://hall.racingmuseum.org/jockey.asp?ID=205

BILL SHOEMAKER

Bill Shoemaker won his first Belmont Stakes in 1957 on Gallant Man.

As THE HORSES WENT to the post for the 1987 Breeders' Cup Classic, the fans at Hollywood Park could hardly contain themselves. They were about to see two Kentucky Derby winners, Ferdinand and Alysheba, duke it out. Of course, Ferdinand's jockey was a whopping fifty-six years old, but the fans were not worried because the jockey was Bill Shoemaker, The Shoe, the nation's winningest jockey. As the race unfolded, Ferdinand and Alysheba engaged in a heart-stopping stretch duel, but Shoemaker didn't touch his whip; he knew Ferdinand disliked it. He hand-rode the horse, to win by less than a nose in one of the most exciting Breeders' Cup races ever.

Born in Texas in 1931, Billie Lee Shoemaker moved to California at age ten. In high school, he boxed and wrestled, but he also started to work with thoroughbreds at the Suzy Q Ranch, where he began cleaning stalls at age fourteen. Later, he worked as an exercise rider. He made his racing debut in March 1949 at age seventeen, winning a month later on Shafter V at Golden Gate Fields, near San Francisco. By the end of 1950, only his second year of riding, he had tied with jockey Joe Culmone to be the nation's leading rider. The Shoe was on his way.

In 1955, aboard Swaps, he beat Nashua to win his first Kentucky Derby. He'd almost lost the mount due to a riding accident the month before. But his agent smuggled him from his hospital bed in California and flew him to Louisville, Kentucky (a ten-hour flight), to ride Swaps in an important prep race.

Even the nation's most talented jockey can make a

mistake, and The Shoe made a dandy one in the 1957 Kentucky Derby on Gallant Man. He misjudged the finish line, standing up early in the irons, or stirrups, and blowing his lead and a victory. But he never misjudged the finish line again and went on to win the Derby three more times, including a 1986 win on Ferdinand at age fifty-four.

In January 1968, a riding accident put Shoemaker in the hospital for three weeks and kept him out of racing for nearly a year. Just a few months after his return, he suffered even more serious injuries when a horse flipped backward on top of him. People around the track figured The Shoe was through as a jockey. But he worked hard to recover and was back racing in four months.

On September 7, 1970, Shoemaker became the winningest jockey of all time, surpassing the record set by Johnny Longden by winning his 6,033rd race on Dares J. Some of those wins came aboard the greatest horses of all time, like Sword Dancer and Damascus, but the Shoe calls Spectacular Bid the greatest horse he ever rode. With Shoemaker in the irons, Spectacular Bid became so unbeatable that in the 1980 Woodward Stakes, no other horses showed up to run against him; he won in a walkover.

When Bill Shoemaker retired in 1990 at the age of fifty-eight, he had won 8,833 races from 40,350 starts. He also had served as president of the Jockeys' Guild. In 1991, he was paralyzed in a car accident, but he worked as a trainer until 1997.

"Shoe had the finest hands in the game," said Eddie Arcaro. "And when a jock has good hands, they can be more effective than a whip. . . . I always thought that you had to make horses run. But not Shoemaker. He got them to run without pushing them."[1]

BILL SHOEMAKER

BORN: August 19, 1931, Fabens, Texas.

FIRST WINNER: Shafter V, April 20, 1949, Golden Gate Fields, California.

HEIGHT: Four feet eleven inches.

IMPORTANT WINS: Kentucky Derby, 1955, 1959, 1965, 1986; Preakness Stakes, 1963, 1967; Belmont Stakes, 1957, 1959, 1962, 1967, 1975; one Breeders' Cup win.

HONORS: Inducted into the National Museum of Racing's Hall of Fame in 1958; Eclipse Award: Outstanding Jockey, 1981; Eclipse Award: Award of Merit, 1981.

Bill Shoemaker (leading) was in his fifties when he won the 1987 Breeders' Cup Classic on Ferdinand.

Internet Address

http://hall.racingmuseum.org/jockey.asp?ID=220

GARY STEVENS

THE DAY BEFORE the 1995 Kentucky Derby, as Gary Stevens was about to board a flight from the St. Louis airport to Louisville, he noticed a boy wearing a brace on his leg. Stevens continued walking, then suddenly stopped and went back to the boy. "What' the matter with you?" he asked the boy. Did he have Perthes disease?

He was not surprised when the boy's mother said yes; Stevens recognized this degenerative bone disease because he'd suffered from it as a boy. In the first and second grades, Stevens had to wear a leg brace for eighteen months. Kids teased him, calling him Ironside, but he didn't let it stop him from doing the things he loved, like playing football and basketball. Today his right leg is two inches shorter than his left, but he believes the experience toughened him.

Stevens told the boy he would be all right, that he'd had the same thing when he was young. "Tomorrow, I'm going to ride in the Kentucky Derby," Stevens told the young boy.[1] He promised that if he won the race, he'd send the boy an autographed photo of himself in the winner's circle.

His mount in the Derby was Thunder Gulch. The colt was so lightly regarded that his odds were 24 to 1. What's more, he was starting from post sixteen, and horses rarely win from such far outer posts. But when the gates flew open, Stevens hustled his colt into perfect striking position just behind the leaders. In the stretch, Thunder Gulch drew away from the competition to win in the sixth-fastest Derby time ever. And Stevens was able to send his young friend a photo.

Stevens has been around horses since his childhood in Idaho. His father was a horse trainer, his mother a champion

GARY STEVENS

Gary Stevens won the 1996 Breeders' Cup Mile on Da Hoss, giving him his fourth Breeders' Cup win.

barrel racer. (Barrel racing is a rodeo sport in which women ride a horse around barrels in a cloverleaf pattern). Gary began riding at age sixteen at Boise's Les Bois Park, where his brother, Scott, was also a jockey. He began winning regularly there and at other tracks in the Northwest. In Portland, where they raced at night, he remembers wearing three pairs of gloves and a snowmobile mask to race in freezing rain. But the weather, and his career, warmed up when he moved to southern California a few years later. By 1986, he was the leading rider on this highly competitive circuit.

His success grew. In 1988, he won the Kentucky Derby aboard Winning Colors, the third filly to ever win the Derby. (A filly is a female horse younger than five years old). Year after year, Stevens ranked among the country's top ten jockeys, in part because he was an extremely hard worker who thought nothing of working sixteen-hour days, seven days a week, with no vacations. By 1995, all that hard work and relentless competition had taken a toll. He was not enjoying himself anymore. In need of a change, he accepted an offer to ride in Hong Kong, where his less strenuous schedule gave him the time to reflect on his career. He realized anew how much he loved his sport.

When he returned home, he found himself enjoying racing again and winning more than ever. He was elected president of the Jockeys' Guild in 1996. In 1997, he won the Kentucky Derby on Silver Charm, in a photo finish. Two weeks later, they won the Preakness Stakes, fending off two powerful rivals to win by a hair. Describing these victories, trainer Richard Mandella commented, "five jumps from the wire he recognized what he was doing wasn't working, and he put in something a little different just to get his nose up. Obviously, there are other great riders . . . but [Stevens] has that last nose down better than anybody I've ever seen."[2]

GARY STEVENS

BORN: March 6, 1963, Caldwell, Idaho.

FIRST WINNER: Lil Star, May 16, 1979, Les Bois Park, Idaho.

HEIGHT: Five feet three inches.

IMPORTANT WINS: Kentucky Derby, 1988, 1995, 1997; Preakness Stakes, 1997; Belmont Stakes, 1995, 1998; six Breeders' Cup wins.

HONORS: Inducted into the National Museum of Racing's Hall of Fame in 1997; Eclipse Award: Outstanding Jockey, 1998.

Stevens and Silver Charm won the 1997 Preakness Stakes by nosing out two talented rivals in a breathtaking finish.

Internet Address

http://hall.racingmuseum.org/jockey.asp?ID=224

CHAPTER NOTES

Eddie Arcaro

1. William Gildea, "Jockey Eddie Arcaro Dead at 81," *The Washington Post*, November 15, 1997, p. D1.

2. Joseph Durso, "Eddie Arcaro, Only Jockey to Win Racing's Triple Crown Twice, Is Dead at 81," *The New York Times*, November 15, 1997, pp. A24, A15.

3. Ibid.

4. Clark Spencer, "Two Triple Crowns Are Unmatched," *The Miami Herald*, November 15, 1997, p. 1D.

Jerry Bailey

1. Frank Luksa, "Jockey Gets a Ride Home at Lone Star," *The Dallas Morning News*, May 30, 1997, p. 1B.

2. "Jerry Bailey," *Keeneland*, n.d., <http://www.keeneland .com/race/bios/jockey/bailey.html> (September 3, 1998).

3. Allen Pusey, "Jerry Bailey: Win or Lose, He's Still an All-Star Jockey," *The Dallas Morning News*, August 31, 1997, p. 1E.

Steve Cauthen

1. Jennie Rees, "A Kid No More, Cauthen Settled, Happy in Roles of Farmer, Father," *The Courier-Journal*, Louisville, Ky., April 26, 1998, p. 1C.

Angel Cordero, Jr.

1. Steve Woodward, "Cordero Rides Off a True Winner," *USA Today*, May 8, 1992, p. 13C.

Pat Day

1. Elizabeth A. Schick, ed., "Pat Day," *Current Biography Yearbook 1997* (New York: H. W. Wilson Company, 1997), p. 132.

2. Jennie Rees, "Pat Day: God Picked Up the Reins; Jockey Found Inspiration at the Breeders' Cup," *The Courier-Journal*, Louisville, Ky., November 5, 1997, p. 1A.

3. "Day Joins 7,000 Club with Win at Saratoga," *Herald-Leader Wire Services*, Lexington Herald-Leader, August 26, 1997, p. C5.

Kent Desormeaux

1. Chuck Culpeper, "'I Feel So Good Inside, So Good:' Kent Desormeaux Complete After Life's Rough Ride," *Lexington Herald-Leader*, May 3, 1998, p. AA4.

2. Andrew Beyer, "Desormeaux: Long Ride to Get Back on Track," *The Washington Post*, May 13, 1998, p. C1.

Julie Krone

1. Julie Krone with Nancy Ann Richards, *Riding for My Life* (Boston: Little, Brown & Company, 1995), p. 68.

2. Andrew Beyer, "Krone's Battle of Body and Soul," *The Washington Post*, March 18, 1995, p. H10.

Isaac Murphy

1. *Spirit of the Times*, New York, June 1890, as quoted by Betty Earle Borries in *Isaac Murphy: Kentucky's Record Jockey* (Berea, Ky.: Kentucke Imprints, 1988), p. 87.

2. Forty-four percent is the generally accepted statistic, based on Murphy's own records.

3. *The Courier-Journal*, Louisville, Ky., May 15, 1891, as quoted by Betty Earle Borries in *Isaac Murphy: Kentucky's Record Jockey* (Berea, Ky.: Kentucke Imprints, 1988), p. 112.

Bill Shoemaker

1. Bill Christine, "Shoe: 'Finest Hands in the Game,'" *Los Angeles Times*, February 2, 1990, p. D1.

Gary Stevens

1. Jim Gintonio, "Double Winner: Stevens Came Up Big Before Derby," *The Phoenix Gazette*, May 9, 1995, p. D1.

2. Jennie Rees, "Gary Stevens: If You Bet Hot Jockey, He's Your Guy; Only Triple Crown Could Make Him Taller in the Saddle," *The Courier-Journal*, Louisville, Ky., June 4, 1997, p. 1A.

INDEX